Tiddlers

Pippa's Painting

by Jill Atkins

Illustrated by Anni Axworthy

W
FRANKLIN WATTS
LONDON•SYDNEY

Notes on the series

TIDDLERS are structured to provide support for children who are starting to read on their own. The stories may also be used for sharing with children.

Starting to read alone can be daunting. **TIDDLERS** help by listing the words in the book for a check before reading, and by providing visual support and repeating words and phrases. These books will both develop confidence and encourage reading and rereading for pleasure.

If you are reading this book with a child, here are a few suggestions:

1. Make reading fun! Choose a time to read when you and the child are relaxed and have time to share the story.
2. Talk about the story before you start reading. Look at the cover and the blurb. What might the story be about? Why might the child like it?
3. Look also at the list of words below - can the child tackle most of the words?
4. Encourage the child to retell the story, using the jumbled picture puzzle.
5. Give praise! Remember that small mistakes need not always be corrected.

Here is a list of the words in this story.

Common words:

a	let	out
and	look	please
can	me	red
green	no	see
I	not	she
is	oh	the

Other words:

blue	painting	rainbow
paint	Pippa	yellow
		yet

Pippa is painting with
red and yellow paint.

She is painting with green and blue paint.

5

"Can I see the painting, Pippa?"

"No, not yet."

"Please can I see it?"

"Not yet."

"Please, Pippa!"

"No!"

"Let me see it!"

"No!"

"Look out!"

"Oh no!"

"Look! It is a rainbow!"

Puzzle Time

a

b

Can you find these pictures in the story?

Which pages are the
pictures from?

Turn over for answers!

Answers

The pictures come from these pages:

a. pages 16-17

b. pages 10-11

c. pages 20-21

d. pages 4-5

First published in 2012 by
Franklin Watts
338 Euston Road
London
NW1 3BH

Franklin Watts Australia
Level 17/207 Kent Street
Sydney NSW 2000

Text © Jill Atkins 2012
Illustration © Anni Axworthy 2012

The rights of Jill Atkins to be
identified as the author and Anni Axworthy
as the illustrator of this Work have been
asserted in accordance with the Copyright,
Designs and Patents Act, 1988.

A CIP catalogue record for this book is
available from the British Library.

ISBN 978 1 4451 0684 7 (hbk)
ISBN 978 1 4451 0690 8 (pbk)

Series Editor: Jackie Hamley
Editor: Melanie Palmer
Series Advisor: Catherine Glavina
Series Designer: Peter Scoulding

Printed in China

Franklin Watts is a division of Hachette Children's Books,
an Hachette UK company. www.hachette.co.uk